Snack Attack

Snack Attack

Stephen Krensky

ILLUSTRATED BY
Stacy Curtis

Ready-to-Read

Simon Spotlight
New York   London   Toronto   Sydney   New Delhi

SIMON SPOTLIGHT

An imprint of Simon & Schuster Children's Publishing Division

1230 Avenue of the Americas, New York, New York 10020

First Simon Spotlight edition April 2012

First Aladdin Paperbacks edition April 2008

Text copyright © 2008 by Stephen Krensky

Illustrations copyright © 2008 by Stacy Curtis

For information about special discounts for bulk purchases, please contact
Simon & Schuster Special Sales at 1-866-506-1949 or
business@simonandschuster.com.

Designed by Sammy Yuen Jr.

The text of this book was set in Futura.

Manufactured in the United States of America 0215 LAK

6 8 10 9 7

Library of Congress Cataloging-in-Publication Data

Krensky, Stephen.

Snack attack / by Stephen Krensky ; illustrated by Stacy Curtis. —
1st Aladdin Paperbacks ed.

p. cm.

Summary: A cat in a shack tricks a rat with a snack.

[1. Cats—Fiction. 2. Rats—Fiction. 3. Stories in rhyme.] I. Curtis, Stacy, ill. II. Title.

PZ8.3.K869Sn 2008

[E]—dc22

ISBN 978-1-4169-0238-6

For Peter, who likes to snack —Stephen Krensky

For Colton —Stacy Curtis

A cat.

A cat and a snack.

A cat and a snack

in a shack.

A rat.

A rat in a crack.

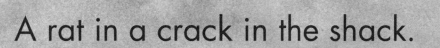

A rat in a crack in the shack.

"Ham and jam!" says the cat.

"What a snack! *Smack, Smack!*"

The rat has a plan.

The rat will attack the
cat for the snack.

Clash!

Crash!

The cat has the rat.

The snack was a trap.

How to
Catch a Rat

The cat has the rat in a sack.

The rat is mad.

But the cat is glad.

For the rat, that is that.

And the cat in the shack gets fat.